# EVIL DEEDS AT RED COUGAR

## BY

## ROBERT E. HOWARD

**British Library Cataloguing-in-Publication Data**
A catalogue record for this book is available from the
British Library

# Robert E. Howard

Robert Ervin Howard was born in Peaster, Texas in 1906. During his youth, his family moved between a variety of Texan boomtowns, and Howard – a bookish and somewhat introverted child – was steeped in the violent myths and legends of the Old South. Although he loved reading and learning, Howard developed a distinctly Texan, hardboiled outlook on the world. He became a passionate fan of boxing, taking it up at an amateur level, and from the age of nine began to write adventure tales of semi-historical bloodshed. In 1919, when Howard was thirteen, his family moved to the Central Texas hamlet of Cross Plains, where he would stay for the rest of his life.

At fifteen Howard began to read the pulp magazines of the day, and to write more seriously. The December 1922 issue of his high school newspaper featured two of his stories, 'Golden Hope Christmas' and 'West is West'. In 1924 he sold his first piece – a short caveman tale titled 'Spear and Fang' – for $16 to the not-yet-famous *Weird Tales* magazine. He published with the magazine regularly over the next few years. 1929 was a breakout year for Howard, in that the 23-year-old writer began to sell to other magazines, such as *Ghost Stories* and *Argosy*, both of whom had previously sent him hundreds of rejection slips. In 1930, he began a correspondence with weird fiction master H. P. Lovecraft which ran up to his death six years later, and is regarded as one of the great correspondence cycles in all of fantasy literature.

It was partly due to Lovecraft's encouragement that Howard created his most famous character, Conan the Cimmerian. Conan – a barbarian-turned-King during the Hyborian Age, a mythical period of some 12,000 years ago – featured in seventeen *Weird Tales* stories between 1933 and 1936, and is now regarded as having spawned the 'sword and sorcery' genre, making Howard's influence on fantasy literature comparable to that of J. R. R. Tolkien's. The Conan stories have since been adapted many times, most famously in the series of films starring Arnold Schwarzenegger.

Howard was enjoying an all-time high in sales by the beginning of 1936, but he was also deeply upset by the ill health of his mother, who had fallen into a coma. On the morning of June 11, 1936, he asked an attending nurse whether she would ever recover, and the nurse replied negatively. Howard walked to his car, parked outside the family home in Cross Plains, and shot himself. He died eight hours later, aged just thirty.

I BEEN ACCUSED OF prejudice agen the town of Red Cougar, on account of my habit of avoiding it if I have to ride fifty miles outen my way to keep from going through there. I denies the slander. It ain't no more prejudiced for me to ride around Red Cougar than it is for a lobo to keep his paw out of a jump-trap. My experiences in that there lair of iniquity is painful to recall. I was a stranger and took in. I was a sheep for the fleecing, and if some of the fleecers got their fingers catched in the shears, it was their own fault. If I shuns Red Cougar like a plague, that makes it mutual, because the inhabitants of Red Cougar shuns me with equal enthusiasm, even to the p'int of deserting their wagons and taking to the bresh if they happen to meet me on the road.

I warn't intending to go there in the first place. I been punching cows over in Utah and was heading for Bear Creek, with the fifty bucks a draw poker game had left me outa my wages. When I seen a trail branching offa the main road I knowed it turnt off to Red Cougar, but it didn't make no impression on me.

But I hadn't gone far past it when I heard a hoss running, and the next thing it busted around a bend in the road with foam flying from the bit rings. They was a gal on it, looking back over her shoulder down the road. Jest as she rounded the turn her hoss stumbled and went to its knees, throwing her over its head.

3

I was offa Cap'n Kidd in a instant and catched her hoss before it could run off. I helped her up, and she grabbed holt of me and hollered: "Don't let 'em get me!"

"Who?" I said, taking off my hat with one hand and drawing a .45 with the other'n.

"A gang of desperadoes!" she panted. "They've chased me for five miles! Oh, please don't let 'em get me!"

"They'll tech you only over my dead carcass," I assured her.

She gimme a look which made my heart turn somersets. She had black curly hair and big innercent gray eyes, and she was the purtiest gal I'd saw in a coon's age.

"Oh, thank you!" she panted. "I knowed you was a gent the minute I seen you. Will you help me up onto my hoss?"

"You shore you ain't hurt none?" I ast, and she said she warn't, so I helped her up, and she gathered up her reins and looked back down the road very nervous. "Don't let 'em foller me!" she begged. "I'm goin' on."

"You don't need to do that," I says. "Wait till I exterminate them scoundrels, and I'll escort you home."

But she started convulsively as the distant pound of hoofs reched us, and said: "Oh, I dast not! They mustn't even see me again!"

"But I want to," I said. "Where you live?"

"Red Cougar," says she. "My name's Sue Pritchard. If you happen up that way, drop in."

"I'll be there!" I promised, and she flashed me a dazzling smile and loped on down the road and outa sight up the Red Cougar trail.

SO I SET TO WORK. I USES a rope wove outa buffalo hide, a right smart longer and thicker and stronger'n the average riata because a man my size has got to have a rope to match. I tied said lariat acrost the road about three foot off the ground.

Then I backed Cap'n Kidd into the bushes, and purty soon six men swept around the bend. The first hoss fell over my rope and the others fell over him, and the way they piled up in the road was beautiful to behold. Before you could bat yore eye they was a most amazing tangle of kicking hosses and cussing men. I chose that instant to ride out of the bresh and throw my pistols down on 'em.

"Cease that scandalous langwidge and rise with yore hands up!" I requested, and they done so, but not cheerfully. Some had been kicked right severe by the hosses, and one had pitched over his cayuse's neck and lit on his head, and his conversation warn't noways sensible.

"What's the meanin' of this here hold-up?" demanded a tall maverick with long yaller whiskers.

"Shet up!" I told him sternly. "Men which chases a he'pless gal like a pack of Injuns ain't fittin' for to talk to a white man."

"Oh, so that's it!" says he. "Well, lemme tell yuh--"

"I said shet up!" I roared, emphasizing my request by shooting the left tip offa his mustash. "I don't aim to powwow with no dern women-chasin' coyotes! In my country we'd decorate a live oak with yore carcasses!"

"But you don't--" began one of the others, but Yaller Whiskers profanely told him to shet up.

"Don't yuh see he's one of Ridgeway's men?" snarled he. "He's got the drop on us, but our turn'll come. Till it does, save yore breath!"

"That's good advice," I says. "Onbuckle yore gun-belts and hang 'em on yore saddle-horns, and keep yore hands away from them guns whilst you does it. I'd plumb welcome a excuse to salivate the whole mob of you."

So they done it, and then I fired a few shots under the hosses' feet and stampeded 'em, and they run off down the road the direction they'd come from. Yaller Whiskers and his pals cussed something terrible.

"Better save yore wind," I advised 'em. "You likely got a good long walk ahead of you, before you catches yore cayuses."

"I'll have yore heart's blood for this," raved Yaller Whiskers. "I'll have yore sculp if I have to trail yuh from here to Jedgment Day! Yuh don't know who yo're monkeyin' with."

"And I don't care!" I snorted. "Vamoose!"

They taken out down the road after their hosses, and I shot around their feet a few times to kinda speed 'em on their way. They disappeared down the road in a faint blue haze of profanity, and I turnt around and headed for Red Cougar.

I hoped to catch up with Miss Pritchard before she got to Red Cougar, but she had too good a start and was going at too fast a gait. My heart pounded at the thought of her and my corns begun to ache. It shore was love at first sight.

Well, I'd follered the trail for maybe three miles when I heard guns banging ahead of me. A little bit later I came to where the trail forked and I didn't know which'n led to Red Cougar. Whilst I was setting there wondering which branch to take, I heard hosses running again, and purty soon a couple of men hove in sight, spurring hard and bending low like they was expecting to be shot from behind. When they approached me I seen they had badges onto their vests, and bullet holes in their hats.

"Which is the road to Red Cougar?" I ast perlitely.

"That'n," says the older feller, p'inting back the way they'd come. "But if yo're aimin' to go there I advises yuh to reflect deeply on the matter. Ponder, young man, ponder and meditate! Life is sweet, after all!"

"What you mean?" I ast. "Who're you all chasin'?"

"Chasin' hell!" says he, polishing his sheriff's badge with his sleeve. "We're bein' chased! Buck Ridgeway's in town!"

"Never heard of him," I says.

"Well," says the sheriff, "Buck don't like strangers no more'n he does law-officers. And yuh see how well he likes them!"

"This here's a free country!" I snorted. "When I stays outa town on account of this here Ridgeway or anybody else they'll be ice in hell thick enough for the devil to skate on. I'm goin' to visit a young lady--Miss Sue Pritchard. Can you tell me where she lives?"

They looked at me very pecooliar, and the sheriff says: "Oh, in that case--well, she lives in the last cabin north of the general store, on the left-hand side of the street."

"Le's git goin'," urged his deputy nervously. "They may foller us!"

They started spurring again, and as they rode off, I heard the deputy say: "Reckon he's one of 'em?" And the sheriff said: "If he ain't he's the biggest damn fool that ever lived, to come sparkin' Sue Pritchard--" Then they rode outa hearing. I wondered who they was talking about, but soon forgot it as I rode on into Red Cougar.

I COME IN ON the south end of the town, and it was about like all them little mountain villages. One straggling street, hound dogs sleeping in the dust of the wagon ruts, and a general store and a couple of saloons.

I seen some hosses tied at the hitching rack outside the biggest saloon which said "Mac's Bar" on it, but I didn't see nobody on the streets, although noises of hilarity was coming outa the saloon. I was thirsty and dusty, and I decided I better have me a drink and spruce up some before I called on Miss Pritchard. So I watered Cap'n Kidd at the trough, and tied him to a tree (if I'd tied him to the hitch rack he'd of kicked the tar outa the other hosses) and went into the saloon. They warn't nobody in there but a old coot with gray whiskers tending bar, and the noise was all coming from another room. From the racket I jedged they was a bowling alley in there and the gents was bowling.

I beat the dust outa my pants with my hat and called for whiskey. Whilst I was drinking it the feller said: "Stranger in town, hey?"

I said I was and he said: "Friend of Buck Ridgeway's?"

"Never seen him in my life," says I, and he says: "Then you better git outa town fast as you can dust it. Him and his bunch ain't here--he pulled out jest a little while ago--but Jeff Middleton's in there, and Jeff's plenty bad."

I started to tell him I warn't studying Jeff Middleton, but jest then a lot of whooping bust out in the bowling alley like somebody had made a ten-strike or something, and here

9

come six men busting into the bar whooping and yelling and slapping one of 'em on the back.

"Decorate the mahogany, McVey!" they whooped. "Jeff's buyin'! He jest beat Tom Grissom here six straight games!"

They surged up to the bar and one of 'em tried to jostle me aside, but as nobody ain't been able to do that successful since I got my full growth, all he done was sprain his elbow. This seemed to irritate him, because he turnt around and said heatedly: "What the hell you think yo're doin'?"

"I'm drinkin' me a glass of corn squeezin's," I replied coldly, and they all turnt around and looked at me, and they moved back from the bar and hitched at their pistol-belts. They was a hard looking gang, and the feller they called Middleton was the hardest looking one of 'em.

"Who're you and where'd you come from?" he demanded.

"None of yore damn business," I replied with a touch of old Southern curtesy.

He showed his teeth at this and fumbled at his gun-belt.

"Air you tryin' to start somethin'?" he demanded, and I seen McVey hide behind a stack of beer kaigs.

"I ain't in the habit of startin' trouble," I told him. "All I does is end it. I'm in here drinkin' me a quiet dram when you coyotes come surgin' in hollerin' like you was the first critter which ever hit a pin."

"So you depreciates my talents, hey?" he squalled like he was stung to the quick. "Maybe you think you could beat me, hey?"

"I ain't yet seen the man which could hold a candle to my game," I replied with my usual modesty.

"All right!" he yelled, grinding his teeth. "Come into the alley, and I'll show you some action, you big mountain grizzly!"

"Hold on!" says McVey, sticking his head up from behind the kaigs. "Be keerful, Jeff! I believe that's--"

"I don't keer who he is!" raved Middleton. "He has give me a mortal insult! Come on, you, if you got the nerve!"

"You be careful with them insults!" I roared menacingly, striding into the alley. "I ain't the man to be bulldozed." I was looking back over my shoulder when I shoved the door open with my palm and I probably pushed harder'n I intended to, and that's why I tore the door offa the hinges. They all looked kinda startled, and McVey give a despairing squeak, but I went on into the alley and picked up a bowl ball which I brandished in defiance.

"Here's fifty bucks!" I says, waving the greenbacks. "We puts up fifty each and rolls for five dollars a game. That suit you?"

I couldn't understand what he said, because he jest made a noise like a wolf grabbing a beefsteak, but he snatched up a bulldog, and perjuiced ten five-dollar bills, so I jedged it was agreeable with him.

But he had a awful temper, and the longer we played, the madder he got, and when I had beat him five straight games and taken twenty-five outa his fifty, the veins stood out purple onto his temples.

"It's yore roll," I says, and he throwed his bowl ball down and yelled: "Blast yore soul, I don't like yore style! I'm through and I'm takin' down my stake! You gits no more of my money, damn you!"

"Why, you cheap-heeled piker!" I roared. "I thought you was a sport, even if you was a hoss-thief, but--"

"Don't you call me a hoss-thief!" he screamed.

"Well, cow-thief then," I says. "If yo're so dern particular--"

IT WAS AT THIS INSTANT that he lost his head to the p'int of pulling a pistol and firing at me p'int-blank. He would of ondoubtedly shot me, too, if I hadn't hit him in the head with my bowl ball jest as he fired. His bullet went into the ceiling and his friends begun to display their disapproval by throwing pins and bulldogs at me. This irritated me almost beyond control, but I kept my temper and taken a couple of 'em by the neck and beat their heads together till they was limp. The matter would of ended there, without any vi'lence, but the other three insisted on taking the thing serious, and I defy any man to remain tranquil when three hoss-thieves are kyarving at him with bowies and beating him over the head with ten-pins.

But I didn't intend to bust the big ceiling lamp; I jest hit it by accident with the chair which I knocked one of my enermies stiff with. And it warn't my fault if one of 'em got blood all over the alley. All I done was break his nose and knock out seven teeth with my fist. How'd I know he was going to fall in the alley and bleed on it. As for that section of wall which got knocked out, all I can say is it's a derned flimsy wall which can be wrecked by throwing a man through it. I thought I'd throwed him through a winder until I looked closer and seen it was a hole he busted through the wall. And can I help it if them scalawags blowed holes in the roof till it looked like a sieve trying to shoot me?

It wasn't my fault, nohow.

But when the dust settled and I looked around to see if I'd made a clean sweep, I was jest in time to grab the shotgun which old man McVey was trying to shoot me through the barroom door with.

"You oughta be ashamed," I reproved. "A man of yore age and venerable whiskers, tryin' to shoot a defenseless stranger in the back."

"But my bowlin' alley's wrecked!" he wept, tearing the aforesaid whiskers. "I'm a rooint man! I sunk my wad in it--and now look at it!"

"Aw, well," I says, "it warn't my fault, but I cain't see a honest man suffer. Here's seventy-five dollars, all I got."

"'Tain't enough," says he, nevertheless making a grab for the dough like a kingfisher diving after a pollywog. "'Tain't near enough."

"I'll collect the rest from them coyotes," I says.

"Don't do it!" he shuddered. "They'd kill me after you left!"

"I wanta do the right thing," I says. "I'll work out the rest of it."

He looked at me right sharp then, and says: "Come into the bar."

But I seen three of 'em was coming to, so I hauled 'em up and told 'em sternly to tote their friends out to the hoss trough and bring 'em to. They done so, kinda wabbling on their feet. They acted like they was still addled in the brains, and McVey said it looked to him like Middleton was out for the day, but I told him it was quite common for a man to be like that which has jest had a fifteen-pound bowling ball split in two over his head.

Then I went into the bar with McVey and he poured out the drinks.

"Air you in earnest about workin' out that debt?" says he.

"Sure," I said. "I always pays my debts, by fair means or foul."

"Ain't you Breckinridge Elkins?" says he, and when I says I was, he says: "I thought I rekernized you when them fools was badgerin' you. Look out for 'em. That ain't all of 'em. The whole gang rode into town a hour or so ago and run the sheriff and his deperty out, but Buck didn't stay long. He seen his gal, and then he pulled out for the hills again with four men. They's a couple more besides them you fit hangin' around somewheres. I dunno where."

"Outlaws?" I said, and he said: "Shore. But the local law-force ain't strong enough to deal with 'em, and anyway, most of the folks in town is in cahoots with 'em, and warns 'em if officers from outside come after 'em. They hang out in the hills ordinary, but they come into Red Cougar regular. But never mind them. I was jest puttin' you on yore guard.

"This is what I want you to do. A month ago I was comin' back to Red Cougar with a tidy fortune in gold dust I'd panned back up in the hills, when I was held up and robbed. It warn't one of Ridgeway's men; it was Three-Fingers Clements, a old lone wolf and the wust killer in these parts. He lives by hisself up in the hills and nobody knows where.

"But I jest recent learnt by accident. He sent a message by a sheepherder and the sheepherder got drunk in my saloon and talked. I learnt he's still got my gold, and aims to sneak out with it as soon as he's j'ined by a gang of desperadoes from Tomahawk. It was them the sheepherder was takin' the message to. I cain't git no help from the sheriff; these outlaws has got him plumb buffaloed. I want you to ride up in the hills and git my gold. Of course, if yo're scairt of him--"

"Who said I was scairt of him or anybody else?" I demanded irritably. "Tell me how to git to his hide-out and I'm on my way."

McVey's eyes kinda gleamed, and he says: "Good boy! Foller the trail that leads outa town to the northwest till you come to Diablo Canyon. Foller it till you come to the fifth branch gulch openin' into it on the right. Turn off the trail then and foller the gulch till you come to a big white oak nigh the left-hand wall. Climb up outa the gulch there and head due west up the slope. Purty soon you'll see a crag like a chimney stickin' out above a clump of spruces. At the foot of that crag they's a cave, and Clements is livin' there. And he's a tough old--"

"It's as good as did," I assured him, and had another drink, and went out and clumb aboard Cap'n Kidd and headed out of town.

BUT AS I RODE PAST THE last cabin on the left, I suddenly remembered about Sue Pritchard, and I 'lowed Three Fingers could wait long enough for me to pay my respecks on her. Likely she was expecting me and getting nervous and impatient because I was so long coming. So I reined up to the stoop and hailed, and somebody looked at me through a winder. They also appeared to be a rifle muzzle trained on me, too, but who could blame folks for being cautious with them Ridgeway coyotes in town.

"Oh, it's you!" said a female voice, and then the door opened and Sue Pritchard said: "Light and come in! Did you kill any of them rascals?"

"I'm too soft-hearted for my own good," I says apologetically. "I jest merely only sent 'em down the road on foot. But I ain't got time to come in now. I'm on my way up in the mountains to see Three Fingers Clements. I aimed to stop on my way back, if it's agreeable with you."

"Three Fingers Clements?" says she in a pecooliar voice. "Do you know where he is?"

"McVey told me," I said. "He's got a poke of dust he stole from McVey. I'm goin' after it."

She said something under her breath which I must have misunderstood because I was sure Miss Pritchard wouldn't use the word it sounded like.

"Come in jest a minute," she begged. "You got plenty of time. Come in and have a snort of corn juice. My folks is all visitin' and it gets mighty lonesome to a gal. Please come in!"

Well, I never could resist a purty gal, so I tied Cap'n Kidd to a stump that looked solid, and went in, and she brung out her old man's jug. It was tolerable licker. She said she never drunk none, personal.

We set and talked, and there wasn't a doubt we cottoned to each other right spang off. There is some that says that Breckinridge Elkins hain't got a lick of sense when it comes to wimmin-folks--among these bein' my cousin, Bearfield Buckner--but I vow and declare that same is my only weakness, if any, and that likewise it is manly weakness.

This Sue Pritchard was plumb sensible I seen. She wasn't one of these flighty kind that a feller would have to court with a banjo or geetar. We talked around about bear-traps and what was the best length barrel on shotguns and similar subjects of like nature. I likewise told her one or two of my mild experiences and her eyes boogered big as saucers. We finally got around to my latest encounter.

"Tell me some more about Three Fingers," she coaxed. "I didn't know anybody knowed his hide-out." So I told her what all McVey said, and she was a heap interested, and had me repeat the instructions how to get there two or three times. Then she ast me if I'd met any badmen in town, and I told her I'd met six and they was now recovering on pallets in the back of the general store. She looked startled at this, and purty soon she ast me to excuse her because she heard one of the neighbor women calling her. I didn't hear nobody, but I said all right, and she went out of the back door, and I heard her whistle three times. I sot there and had another snort or so and reflected that the gal was ondoubtedly taken with me.

She was gone quite a spell, and finally I got up and looked out the back winder and seen her standing down by the corral talking to a couple of fellers. As I looked one of 'em got on a bobtailed roan and headed north at a high run, and t'other'n come on back to the cabin with Sue.

"This here's my cousin Jack Montgomery," says she. "He wants to go with you. He's jest a boy, and likes excitement."

He was about the hardest-looking boy I ever seen, and he seemed remarkable mature for his years, but I said: "All right. But we got to git goin'."

"Be careful, Breckinridge," she advised. "You, too, Jack."

"I won't hurt Three Fingers no more'n I got to," I promised her, and we went on our way yonderly, headed for the hideout.

WE GOT TO DIABLO CANYON in about a hour, and went up it about three miles till we come to the gulch mouth McVey had described. All to onst Jack Montgomery pulled up and p'inted down at a pool we was passing in a holler of the rock, and hollered: "Look there! Gold dust scattered at the aidge of the water!"

"I don't see none," I says.

"Light," he urged, getting off his cayuse. "I see it! It's thick as butter along the aidge!"

Well, I got down and bent over the pool but I couldn't see nothing and all to onst something hit me in the back of the head and knocked my hat off. I turnt around and seen Jack Montgomery holding the bent barrel of a Winchester carbine in his hands. The stock was busted off and pieces was laying on the ground. He looked awful surprized about something; his eyes was wild and his hair stood up.

"Air you sick?" I ast. "What you want to hit me for?"

"You ain't human!" he gasped, dropping the bent barrel and jerking out his pistol. I grabbed him and taken it away from him.

"What's the matter with you?" I demanded. "Air you locoed?"

For answer he run off down the canyon shrieking like a lost soul. I decided he must have went crazy like sheepherders does sometimes, so I pursued him and catched him. He fit and hollered like a painter.

"Stop that!" I told him sternly. "I'm yore friend. It's my duty to yore cousin to see that you don't come to no harm."

"Cousin, hell!" says he with frightful profanity. "She ain't no more my cousin than you be."

"Pore feller," I sighed, throwing him on his belly and reaching for his lariat. "Yo're outa yore head and sufferin' from hallucernations. I knowed a sheepherder jest like you onst, only he thought he was Sittin' Bull."

"What you doin'?" he hollered, as I started tying him with his rope.

"Don't you worry," I soothed him. "I cain't let you go tearin' around over these mountains in yore condition. I'll fix you so's you'll be safe and comfortable till I git back from Three Fingers' cave. Then I'll take you to Red Cougar and we'll send you to some nice, quiet insane asylum."

"Blast yore soul!" he shrieked. "I'm sane as you be! A damn sight saner, because no man with a normal brain could ignore gittin' a rifle stock broke off over his skull like you done!"

Whereupon he tries to kick me between the eyes and otherwise give evidence of what I oncet heard a doctor call his derangement. It was a pitiful sight to see, especially since he was a cousin to Miss Sue Pritchard and would ondoubtedly be my cousin-in-law one of these days. He jerked and rassled and some of his words was downright shocking.

But I didn't pay no attention to his ravings. I always heard the way to get along with crazy people was to humor 'em. I was afeared if I left him laying on the ground the wolves might chaw him, so I tied him up in the crotch of a big tree where they couldn't rech him. I likewise tied his hoss by the pool where it could drink and graze.

"Lissen!" Jack begged as I clumb onto Cap'n Kidd. "I give up! Ontie me and I'll spill the beans! I'll tell you everything!"

"You jest take it easy," I soothed. "I'll be back soon."

"$#%&*@!" says he, frothing slightly at the mouth.

With a sigh of pity I turnt up the gulch, and his langwidge till I was clean outa sight ain't to be repeated. A mile or so on I come to the white oak tree, and clumb outa the gulch and went up a long slope till I seen a jut of rock like a chimney rising above the trees. I slid offa Cap'n Kidd and drawed my pistols and snuck for'ard through the thick bresh till I seen the mouth of a cave ahead of me. And I also seen something else, too.

A man was laying in front of it with his head in a pool of blood.

I rolled him over and he was still alive. His sculp was cut open, but the bone didn't seem to be caved in. He was a lanky old coot, with reddish gray whiskers, and he didn't have but three fingers onto his left hand. They was a pack tore up and scattered on the ground nigh him, but I reckon the pack mule had run off. They was also hoss-tracks leading west.

They was a spring nearby and I brung my hat full of water and sloshed it into his face, and tried to pour some into his mouth, but it warn't no go. When I throwed the water over him he kinda twitched and groaned, but when I tried to pour the water down his gullet he kinda instinctively clamped his jaws together like a bulldog.

Then I seen a jug setting in the cave, so I brung it out and pulled out the cork. When it popped he opened his mouth convulsively and reched out his hand.

So I poured a pint or so down his gullet, and he opened his eyes and glared wildly around till he seen his busted pack, and then he clutched his whiskers and shrieked: "They got it! My poke of dust! I been hidin' up here for weeks, and jest when I was goin' to make a jump for it, they finds me!"

"Who?" I ast.

"Buck Ridgeway and his gang!" he squalled. "I was keerless. When I heard hosses I thought it was the men which was comin' to help me take my gold out. Next thing I knowed Ridgeway's bunch had run outa the bresh and was beatin' me over the head with their Colts. I'm a rooint man!"

"Hell's fire!" quoth I with passion. Them Ridgeways was beginning to get on my nerves. I left old man Clements howling his woes to the skies like a timber wolf with the bellyache, and I forked Cap'n Kidd and headed west. They'd left a trail the youngest kid on Bear Creek could foller.

IT LED FOR FIVE MILES through as wild a country as I ever seen outside the Humbolts, and then I seen a cabin ahead, on a wide benchland and that backed agen a steep mountain slope. I could jest see the chimney through the tops of a dense thicket. It warn't long till sun-down and smoke was coming outa the chimney.

I knowed it must be the Ridgeway hideout, so I went busting through the thicket in sech a hurry that I forgot they might have a man on the look-out. I'm powerful absent minded thataway. They was one all right, but I was coming so fast he missed me with his buffalo gun, and he didn't stop to reload but run into the cabin yelling: "Bar the door quick! Here comes the biggest man in the world on the biggest hoss in creation!"

They done so. When I emerged from amongst the trees they opened up on me through the loop-holes with sawed-off shotguns. If it'd been Winchesters I'd of ignored 'em, but even I'm a little bashful about buckshot at close range, when six men is shooting at me all to onst. So I retired behind a big tree and begun to shoot back with my pistols, and the howls of them worthless critters when my bullets knocked splinters in their faces was music to my ears.

They was a corral some distance behind the cabin with six hosses in it. To my surprise I seen one of 'em was a bob-tailed roan the feller was riding which I seen talking with Sue Pritchard and Jack Montgomery, and I wondered if them blame outlaws had captured him.

But I warn't accomplishing much, shooting at them loop-holes, and the sun dipped lower and I began to get mad. I decided to rush the cabin anyway and to hell with their derned buckshot, and I dismounted and stumped my toe right severe on a rock. It always did madden me to stump my toe, and I uttered some loud and profane remarks, and I reckon them scoundrels must of thunk I'd stopped some lead, the way they whooped. But jest then I had a inspiration. A big thick smoke was pouring outa the rock chimney so I knowed they was a big fire on the fireplace where they was cooking supper, and I was sure they warn't but one door in the cabin. So I taken up the rock which was about the size of a ordinary pig and throwed it at the chimney.

Boys on Bear Creek is ashamed if they have to use more'n one rock on a squirrel in a hundred-foot tree acrost the creek, and I didn't miss. I hit her center and she buckled and come crashing down in a regular shower of rocks, and most of 'em fell down into the fireplace as I knowed by the way the sparks flew. I jedged that the coals was scattered all over the floor, and the chimney hole was blocked so the smoke couldn't get out that way. Anyway, the smoke begun to pour outa the winders and the Ridgewayers stopped shooting and started hollering.

Somebody yelled: "The floor's on fire! Throw that bucket of water on it!" And somebody else shrieked: "Wait, you damn fool! That ain't water, it's whiskey!"

But he was too late; I heard the splash and then a most amazing flame sprung up and licked outa the winders and the fellers hollered louder'n ever and yelled: "Lemme out! I got smoke in my eyes! I'm chokin' to death!"

I left the thicket and run to the door just as a man throwed it open and staggered out blind as a bat and cussing and shooting wild. I was afeared he'd hurt hisself if he kept tearing around like that, so I taken his shotgun away from him and bent the barrel over his head to kinda keep him quiet, and then I seen to my surprize that he was the feller which rode the bob-tailed roan. I thunk how surprized Sue'd be to know a friend of her'n was a cussed outlaw.

I then went into the cabin which was so full of smoke and gun-powder fumes a man couldn't hardly see nothing. The walls and roof was on fire by now, and them idjits was tearing around with their eyes full of smoke trying to find the door, and one of 'em run head-on into the wall and knocked hisself stiff. I throwed him outside, and got hold of another'n to lead him out, and he cut me acrost the boozum with his bowie. I was so stung by this ingratitude that when I tossed him out to safety I maybe throwed him further'n I aimed to, and it appears they was a stump which he hit his head on. But I couldn't help it being there.

I THEN TURNT AROUND and located the remaining three, which was fighting with each other evidently thinking they was fighting me. Jest as I started for 'em a big log fell outa the roof and knocked two of 'em groggy and sot their clothes on fire, and a regular sheet of flame sprung up and burnt off most of my hair, and whilst I was dazzled by it the surviving outlaw run past me out the door, leaving his smoking shirt in my hand.

Well, I dragged the other two out and stomped on 'em to put out the fire, and the way they hollered you'd of thought I was injuring 'em instead of saving their fool lives.

"Shet up and tell me where the gold is," I ordered, and one of 'em gurgled: "Ridgeway's got it!"

I ast which'n of 'em was him and they all swore they wasn't, and I remembered the feller which run outa the cabin. So I looked around and seen him jest leading a hoss outa the corral to ride off bareback.

"You stop!" I roared, letting my voice out full, which I seldom does. The acorns rattled down outa the trees, and the tall grass bent flat, and the hoss Ridgeway was fixing to mount got scairt and jerked away from him and bolted, and the other hosses knocked the corral gate down and stampeded. Three or four of 'em run over Ridgeway before he could git outa the way.

He jumped up and headed out acrost the flat on foot, wabbling some but going strong. I could of shot him easy but I was afeared he'd hid the gold somewheres, and if I kilt him he couldn't tell me where. So I run and got my lariat and taken out after him on foot, because I figgered he'd duck into the thick bresh to get away. But when he seen I was overhauling him he made for the mountain side and began to climb a steep slope.

I follered him, but before he was much more'n half way up he taken refuge on a ledge behind a dead tree and started shooting at me. I got behind a boulder about seventy-five foot below him, and ast him to surrender, like a gent, but his only reply was a direct slur on my ancestry and more bullets, one of which knocked off a sliver of rock which gouged my neck.

This annoyed me so much that I pulled my pistols and started shooting back at him. But all I could hit was the tree, and the sun was going down and I was afeared if I didn't get him before dark he'd manage to sneak off. So I stood up, paying no attention to the slug he put in my shoulder, and swang my lariat. I always uses a ninety-foot rope; I got no use for them little bitsy pieces of string most punchers uses.

I throwed my noose and looped that tree, and sot my feet solid and heaved, and tore the dern tree up by the roots. But them roots went so deep most of the ledge come along with 'em, and that started a landslide. The first thing I knowed here come the tree and Ridgeway and several tons of loose rock and shale, gathering weight and speed as they come. It sounded like thunder rolling down the mountain, and Ridgeway's screams was frightful to hear. I jumped out from behind the boulder intending to let the landslide split on me and grab him out as it went past me, but I stumbled and fell and that dern tree hit me behind the ear and the next thing I knowed I was traveling down the mountain with Ridgeway and the rest of the avalanche. It was very humiliating.

I was right glad at the time, I recollect, that Miss Sue Pritchard wasn't nowheres near to witness this catastrophe. It's hard for a man to keep his dignity, I found, when he's scootin' in a hell-slue of trees and bresh and rocks and dirt, and I become aware, too, that a snag had tore the seat outa my pants, which made me some despondent. This, I figgered, is what a man gets for losing his self-control. I recollected another time or two when I'd exposed myself to the consequences by exertin' my full strength, and I made me a couple of promises then and there.

It's all right for a single young feller to go hellin' around and let the chips fall where they may, but it's different with a man like me who was almost just the same as practically married. You got to look before you leap, was the way I reckoned it. A man's got to think of his wife and children.

We brung up at the foot of the slope in a heap of boulders and shale, and I threw a few hundred pounds of busted rocks offa me and riz up and shaken the blood outa my eyes and looked around for Ridgeway.

I presently located a boot sticking outa the heap, and I laid hold onto it and hauled him out and he looked remarkable like a skint rabbit. About all the clothes he had left onto him beside his boots was his belt, and I seen a fat buckskin poke stuck under it. So I dragged it out, and about that time he sot up groggy and looked around dizzy and moaned feeble: "Who the hell are you?"

"Breckinridge Elkins, of Bear Creek," I said.

"And with all the men they is in the State of Nevada," he says weakly, "I had to tangle with you. What you goin' to do?"

"I think I'll turn you and yore gang over to the sheriff," I says. "I don't hold much with law--we ain't never had none on Bear Creek--but sech coyotes as you all don't deserve no better."

"A hell of a right you got to talk about law!" he said fiercely. "After plottin' with Badger McVey to rob old man Clements! That's all I done!"

"What you mean?" I demanded. "Clements robbed McVey of this here dust--"

"Robbed hell!" says Ridgeway. "McVey is the crookedest cuss that ever lived, only he ain't got the guts to commit robbery hisself. Why, Clements is a honest miner, the old jackass, and he panned that there dust up in the hills. He's been hidin' for weeks, scairt to try to git outa the country, we was huntin' him too industrious."

"McVey put me up to committin' robbery?" I ejaculated, aghast.

"That's jest what he did!" declared Ridgeway, and I was so overcome by this perfidy that I was plumb paralyzed.

Before I could recover Ridgeway give a convulsive flop and rolled over into the bushes and was gone in a instant.

THE NEXT THING I KNOWED I heard hosses running and I turnt in time to see a bunch of men riding up on me. Old man Clements was with 'em, and I rekernized the others as the fellers I stopped from chasing Sue Pritchard on the road below Red Cougar.

I reched for a pistol, but Clements yelled: "Hold on! They're friends!" He then jumped off and grabbed the poke outa my limp hand and waved it at them triumphantly. "See that?" he hollered. "Didn't I tell you he was a friend? Didn't I tell you he come up here to bust up that gang? He got my gold back for me, jest like I said he would!" He then grabbed my hand and shaked it energetic, and says: "These is the men I sent to Tomahawk for, to help me git my gold out. They got to my cave jest a while after you left. They're prejudiced agen you, but--"

"No, we ain't!" denied Yaller Whiskers, which I now seen was wearing a deputy's badge. And he got off and shaken my hand heartily. "You didn't know we was special law-officers, and I reckon it did look bad, six men chasin' a woman. We thought you was a outlaw! We was purty mad at you when we finally caught our hosses and headed back. But I begun to wonder about you when we found them six disabled outlaws in the store at Red Cougar. Then when we got to Clements' cave, and found you'd befriended him, and had lit out on Ridgeway's trail, it looked still better for you, but I still thought maybe you was after that gold on yo're own account. But, of course, I see now I was all wrong, and I apolergizes. Where's Ridgeway?"

"He got away," I said.

"Never mind!" says Clements, pumping my hand again. "Kirby here and his men has got Jeff Middleton and five more men in the jail at Red Cougar. McVey, the old hypocrite, taken to the hills when Kirby rode into town. And we got six more of Ridgeway's gang tied up over at Ridgeway's cabin--or where it was till you burnt it down. They're shore a battered mob! It musta been a awful fight! You look like you been through a tornado yoreself. Come on with us and our prisoners to Tomahawk. I buys you a new suit of clothes, and we celebrates!"

"I got to git a feller I left tied up in a tree down the gulch," I said. "Jack Montgomery. He's et loco weed or somethin'. He's crazy."

They laughed hearty, and Kirby says: "You got a great sense of humor, Elkins. We found him when we come up the gulch, and brung him on with us. He's tied up with the rest of 'em back there. You shore was slick, foolin' McVey into tellin' you where Clements was hidin', and foolin' that whole Ridgeway gang into thinkin' you aimed to rob Clements! Too bad you didn't know we was officers, so we could of worked together. But I gotta laugh when I think how McVey thought he was gyppin' you into stealin' for him, and all the time you was jest studyin' how to rescue Clements and bust up Ridgeway's gang! Haw! Haw! Haw!"

"But I didn't--" I begun dizzily, because my head was swimming.

"You jest made one mistake," says Kirby, "and that was when you let slip where Clements was hidin'."

"But I never told nobody but Sue Pritchard!" I says wildly.

"Many a good man has been euchered by a woman," says Kirby tolerantly. "We got the whole yarn from Montgomery. The minute you told her, she snuck out and called in two of Ridgeway's men and sent one of 'em foggin' it to tell Buck where to find Clements, and she sent the other'n, which was Montgomery, to go along with you and lay you out before you could git there. She lit for the hills when we come into Red Cougar and I bet her and Ridgeway are streakin' it over the mountains together right now. But that ain't yore fault. You didn't know she was Buck's gal."

The perfidity of wimmen!

"Gimme my hoss," I said groggily. "I been scorched and shot and cut and fell on by a avalanche, and my honest love has been betrayed. You sees before you the singed, skint and blood-soaked result of female treachery. Fate has dealt me the joker. My heart is busted and the seat is tore outa my pants. Git outa the way. I'm ridin'."

"Where to?" they ast, awed.

"Anywhere," I bellers, "jest so it's far away from Red Cougar."